# THE BEASTS OF
# BOGGART HOLLOW

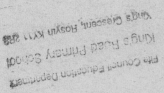

# The Beasts of Boggart Hollow

Andrew Matthews

Illustrated by Chris Fisher

Orion
Children's Books

for
Rose and Jacob

First published in Great Britain in 1996
by Orion Children's Books
a division of the Orion Publishing Group Ltd
Orion House
5 Upper St Martin's Lane
London WC2H 9EA

This edition published 2006 for Index Books Limited

Text copyright © Andrew Matthews 1996
Illustrations copyright © Chris Fisher 1996

The right of Andrew Matthews and Chris Fisher to be identified as the
author and illustrator respectively of this work has been asserted.

A catalogue record for this book is
available from the British Library

Printed in Great Britain by
Clays Ltd, St Ives plc

ISBN 1 85881 270 2 (HB)
ISBN 1 85881 192 9 (PB)

# Contents

# Introduction

A bit longer than a long time ago, there was a village called Boggart Hollow. It lay in a secret valley, miles from anywhere. In fact, the valley was so secret that hardly anybody visited the place, and it was left off all the maps.

The people who lived in Boggart Hollow grew fed up with having no visitors. Nothing exciting ever happened there, and the villagers eventually ran out of jokes and stories to tell one another during the long winter nights. One by one, the houses and cottages fell empty, until at last the place lay deserted.

Then something peculiar happened. Animals made their homes in the village. Living in houses made the animals more like people, and before long they started to do the things that people used to do. Smoke curled out of the bakery chimney, lights shone in the windows at night and front gardens became neat and trim again.

Of course, the animals couldn't get everything right, but they managed very well. In time, they forgot all about the world outside, and the world forgot all about them. If any humans stumbled across Boggart Hollow by mistake, they couldn't believe what they saw there — and no one else believed them when they spoke about it afterwards. The stories they told became mixed up, and then written down in books that nobody ever read ... until now.

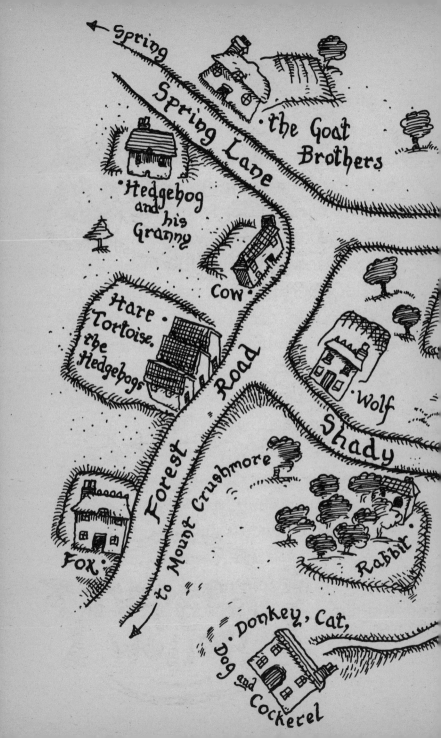

# 1

# How the Beasts Came to Boggart Hollow

The last person to live in Boggart Hollow was Ned Flowers. Ned was a stubborn, cantankerous sort of chap with mean eyes and a chin that was bristly enough to rasp the paint off a door. He'd always been a bit of a rogue, but when he found himself alone in the village he went from bad to worse and turned to a life of crime.

Before long, Ned fell into the company of two other villains, Tinkin Crab and Jimmy Jemmy. They formed a gang, and robbed rich merchants on their way to market. Boggart Hollow made a perfect hideout because no one knew it was there, so no one could find them.

The gang lived in a woodcutter's cottage at the edge of the village, and they whiled away the evenings by counting their ill-gotten gains and telling one another the most frightening stories they could think of. They might have stayed there for years and years if it hadn't been for the Animal Choir.

It all happened like this . . .

A few miles away from Boggart Hollow was the village of Much Hassett. Farmer Barnes lived there with his wife and family. On the farm there was a donkey who was so old that everybody had forgotten his name and just called him Donkey. One day, Farmer Barnes was out in the yard with his wife, and Donkey heard them talking.

"Donkey's good for nothing these days,"

said Farmer Barnes. "He's too old to carry heavy loads."

"He's not worth the feed we give him," Mrs Barnes said. "We'd better get rid of him."

When Donkey heard this, his long ears twirled round and round. "Get rid of me?" he said. "After all the years of hard work I've put into the farm? I won't be thrown out! I've still got a good loud voice, so I'll run away and be a singer instead."

That night, while the farmer and his family were fast asleep, Donkey crept out of the stables and clopped off down the road.

At dawn, Donkey met a cat who was yowling at the roadside.

"What's the matter?" Donkey asked.

"My owners threw me out because I'm too old to catch mice any more," said Cat. "All I want to do is lap cream and sleep all day."

"Humans are so ungrateful!" said Donkey. "Why don't you come with me? I'm going to earn my fortune as a singer, and I'm sure our voices would go together perfectly."

So Cat and Donkey became friends, and walked along the road together.

At noon, they met a dog who was howling pitifully beside a sign post.

"You seem a bit down in the dumps, mate," said Donkey. "What's wrong?"

"Humans," Dog replied. "When I was a puppy, my owners made a great fuss of me, but now I'm old they don't want me any more. They chucked me out of the house like an old boot."

"What a rotten lot!" Donkey said sympathetically. "Why don't you come with Cat and me? We're going to be singers, and I'm sure that with that howl of yours, we could make beautiful music together."

So Dog joined Cat
and Donkey on
their journey.

Just before sunset, the three friends met a
cockerel, perched on a stile, crowing fit to
burst.

"You look miserable, chum," said
Donkey. "What's up?"

"I worked on a farm all my life,"
Cockerel explained. "Every morning, I
crowed my loudest to wake the farmer up
in time for work. Now he's got a clock, he
doesn't need me any more. I heard him say
that he was going to pop me into a pot to
make a stew."

"That's terrible!" cried Donkey. "Come with
us. You've got a fine voice, and it's just
what we need to make our choir complete."

So Cockerel joined Dog, Cat and Donkey.

None of the animals had ever been so far away from their homes before, and after night fell they lost their way. They entered a thick forest and wandered about for hours until they were all tired, hungry and thirsty.

Then Cat, who had sharp eyes, spotted a glimmer of light between the trees, and the animals made their way towards it. The light was shining from the window of a small cottage. Through the window, the animals could see three men, seated round a table that was piled high with good things to eat.

"What I wouldn't give for a nice juicy fish head!" mewed Cat.

"Or a few crunchy bones!" whined Dog.

"Or just a handful of corn!" clucked Cockerel.

"We'll all get something to eat, you mark my words!" said Donkey. "We'll sing for our supper. Those men will be so thrilled by our Animal Choir that they'll invite us in for a meal."

Now it so happened that the three men in the cottage were Ned Flowers and his gang. Ned was spinning a yarn about a weird creature that haunted the forest. Tinkin Crab was so frightened that his hair was standing on end, and Jimmy Jemmy's teeth went clickety-clack as they chattered together.

"The creature's got eyes like slimy pools, and long black claws," Ned said in a deep, dark voice. "Its teeth are sharper than bits of broken glass."

"W-what does it eat, Ned?" Tinkin squeaked.

"People," said Ned. "It hunts them through the forest at night, and when it finds them, it lets out a blood-tingling roar that sounds like —"

At that moment, Donkey brayed, Cat yowled, Dog howled and Cockerel crowed together. It made a terrible racket.

"It's — IT!" screamed Jimmy, and he was off out through the door as fast as he could run, with Tinkin close behind him. Ned ran after them. He'd forgotten that the creature was imaginary, and he was just as scared as the others.

The Animal Choir stopped singing and stared at one another in astonishment.

"Where did they go?" said Cockerel.

"Perhaps they were so impressed they've rushed off to tell their friends," Donkey said.

The animals approached the cottage curiously, and found the front door wide open.

"They must want us to go in and help ourselves to the food!" said Donkey. "Maybe humans aren't so bad after all."

The Animal Choir entered the cottage, and were soon tucking into a fine feast. After they had finished it, they put out the lamps and settled down for the night. Cat curled up on a shelf near the window, Dog stretched out in front of the fire, Donkey knelt down in the corner and Cockerel went to roost on the roof.

Meanwhile, deep in the forest, Ned Flowers had begun to get over his fright. "We've made proper fools of ourselves!" he said. "There's no such thing as the Creature of the Forest."

"Oh no?" said Tinkin. "What made that row, then?"

"I don't know, but I'm going back to find out," Ned said. "Who's coming with me?"

"Not me!" snorted Tinkin. "Me neither!" said Jimmy.

Muttering and grumbling to himself, Ned went back to the cottage. When he saw that the lamps were out, he guessed that someone must be inside, so he sneaked round the back, slid the window open and climbed in. The cottage was darker than the inside of a sack of soot, and as Ned stretched out his hands to feel his way, he caught hold of Cat's tail.

Cat woke up and gave Ned a nasty scratch on his face. Ned shouted with pain, and that woke up Dog and Donkey. Dog sank his teeth into Ned's left leg, and Donkey gave the robber such a hefty kick that he went flying out through the open window. All the rumpus woke Cockerel, who shouted,

"Cock-a-doodle-doo! Cock-a-doodle-doo!" at the top of his voice.

Ned picked himself up and ran off through the forest as though the seat of his pants had caught fire. He didn't stop running until he found Tinkin and Jimmy.

"The cottage has been taken over by another gang!" Ned panted. "There's a witch with long nails — she scratched my face, then someone stabbed me in the leg and gave me a whack with a heavy club. Worst of all, there's a giant as tall as a house. As I was running away, I heard him shouting - *Cut the crook in two! Cut the crook in two!* I think they're still following me."

So Ned and his gang fled the forest, and they never dared to go near Boggart Hollow again.

As for the Animal Choir, they decided to settle in the cottage, and they became the first beasts of Boggart Hollow. They were so respected by the other animals who came to the village that Donkey was made mayor, Cat became his assistant, Dog was given the post of night-watchman, and Cockerel made a wonderful town crier. They were so busy that they never had time to sing as a choir, which was just as well — the noise would have frightened the young animals out of their wits.

# 2

# The Rat Wedding

At the end of Hall Avenue stood a ruined mansion where the squire of Boggart Hollow once lived. When Mr and Mrs Rat moved into the mansion with their daughter Rita, Mrs Rat was delighted. "We can't mix with riff-raff now we live here," she told her husband. "It wouldn't suit the neighbourhood." And she set about teaching Rita good manners.

"Whenever you gnaw a piece of mouldy cheese, Rita, be sure to hold out your little claws," said Mrs Rat. "And never let your tail dangle over the edge of a dustbin when you're inside, it's not polite."

Rita soon grew tired of her mother's fussy ways, but she did as she was told and never once complained.

So it came as a great shock when one day Rita walked into the dining room arm in arm with a young male rat. "This is Ricky, Mother!" she said. "We want to get married!"

"Married?" cried Mrs Rat, twiddling her whiskers. She lifted her head and looked haughtily down her nose at Ricky. "Have you come here to ask for my daughter's paw in marriage?" she demanded.

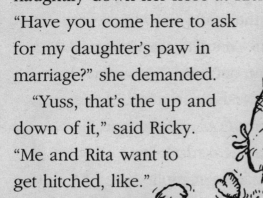

"Yuss, that's the up and down of it," said Ricky. "Me and Rita want to get hitched, like."

"I'm afraid that's quite impossible!" said Mrs Rat.

"My daughter moves in the highest society, and you wouldn't make a suitable husband at all!"

"But he's lovely!" Rita wailed. "He can squeak and scamper like anything, and his tail is as slithery as a snake."

"There's more to marriage than a slithery tail," said Mrs Rat.

And that was that. No matter how Rita wept, or how Mr Rat pleaded with her to change her mind, Mrs Rat stayed firm. "I won't have my daughter marrying someone common!" she declared. "As a matter of fact, I have someone in mind — one of the highest people in the land."

"Who's that?" asked Mr Rat.

"The sun," Mrs Rat replied. "It's noon, so he should be right overhead. Let's go into the garden and speak to him."

The sun was high in the sky, shining down on the trees and flowers. He noticed the rats staring up at him, and he smiled at them in a polite sort of way. "Good afternoon," he said.

"Mr Sun," said Mrs Rat. "I'll come straight to the point. You're famous the world over, and your strength is second to none. I'm pleased to tell you that I've decided you should be Rita's husband!"

"Me, strong?" said the sun. "See that cloud over there? When he floats across my face, everything goes dark. He's far stronger than I am. He's the one you're looking for."

The cloud was alarmed when he heard this. He loved being free, and sailing across the sky, and he didn't want to marry anyone — especially a rat.

"I'm not strong at all!" he said quickly. "I'm a real wimp compared to the wind. As soon as he blows, I go flying all over the place. The wind is the one you should be talking to."

The wind happened to be in the garden at that very moment. He was rattling the leaves on the trees and making the flowers nod their heads.

"Mr Wind," said Mrs Rat. "Mr Cloud, who is far stronger than Mr Sun, tells me that you are stronger than he is, so you must marry my daughter!"

"Strong?" said the wind. "I'm useless compared to your old garden wall. If you stand behind him when I'm blowing my hardest, you won't feel a thing."

At this, Rita burst into tears and stamped

her paws on the ground. "I don't care what you say, Mother," she sobbed, "I'm *not* getting married to the garden wall!"

"You won't have to, don't you worry," said the wall. "I might look pretty solid and reliable, but take a look at that big hole in my middle. That was made by someone far stronger than I am."

"Who?" said Mrs Rat.

"Why, Ricky Rat, of course!" chuckled the wall. "He dug his way right through me so he could meet Rita secretly in the garden. A rat is the strongest thing in the world — everybody knows that!"

And so Rita and Ricky were married, and

Mrs Rat invited all her posh friends to the wedding feast.

"My dear," one of them said to her, "wherever did you find Rita such a fine young husband."

"Some very important friends of ours told us about him," said Mrs Rat. "We were thinking of marrying Rita to the sun, but of course, Ricky is *so* much stronger!"

# 3

# Rabbit and the Wind

The rats weren't the only beasts of Boggart Hollow that the wind had trouble with, because one day it got into a bit of a barney with Rabbit.

Rabbit seemed harmless enough. With his lop ears and his thick, soft fur, Rabbit looked gentle and sweet-natured, but he was cross-tempered, quarrelsome and greedy.

Rabbit lived with his wife in Shady Lane. Their house was built of bricks, and had a big back garden. The garden was Rabbit's pride and joy. There were no flowers in it, not so much as a daisy, for Rabbit was only interested in growing things that he liked to eat.

One morning in late summer, Rabbit went out into the garden for a gloat over his fruit and vegetables. "What a lot of crunching and munching there'll be at harvest time!" he said to himself. "I'll be able to scoff myself silly."

But when he got outside, Rabbit had a nasty shock. The wind had been in his garden the night before and had played a game of rough and tumble with his plants. He had knocked over Rabbit's peas and beans, and shaken his apple and plum trees so hard that a whole load of fruit lay spoiled on the ground.

Rabbit was furious. He drummed the ground with his back paws, flounced his tufty tail and hurried inside to tell his wife what had happened. "The wind's going to pay for this," he told her angrily.

Rabbit stormed out through the front door, and saw that the wind was bending the branches and whispering in the leaves of the trees on the other side of the road.

"I want a word with you, Wind!" snapped Rabbit.

"What's your problem?" the wind said dreamily.

"You are!" said Rabbit. "You were in my garden last night, and you ruined it."

"Oh dear!" the wind said bashfully. "Perhaps I did get a little carried away. I am sorry."

"Sorry won't do," said Rabbit. "I know my rights! I demand compensation for my fruit and vegetables."

"You're quite right," the wind said. "I get about the world quite a bit, and I've picked up some interesting items on my travels. Let me think for a moment . . .Ah! I know!"

There was a swooshing sound, and a tatty tablecloth flapped out of nowhere. It landed on the ground in front of Rabbit.

"That should do it," said the wind.

"What?" cried Rabbit. "There's no crunching or munching in this!"

"You don't understand," the wind said. "It's a magic tablecloth. All you have to do is say - *Tablecloth, spread!* - and it will serve you with a feast of your favourite food."

"You must take me for a fool!" Rabbit sneered.

"Try it if you don't believe me," the wind told him.

Rabbit cleared his throat and said, "Tablecloth, spread!" Straight away, the tablecloth unscrumpled itself, and there were bowls of crispy salad, radishes as big as apples, and carrots as long as summer afternoons.

Rabbit plonked himself down and polished off the lot. He didn't save a scrap for his wife, he only thought of himself.

"Happy now?" asked the wind.

"Right as ninepence!" Rabbit said, with a loud burp.

The wind went off on his way, and Rabbit rolled up the magic tablecloth. He took it into the house to show his wife.

Mrs Rabbit listened patiently to what her husband told her about the wind and the tablecloth, but just as he was opening his mouth to say, "Tablecloth, spread!" she interrupted him.

"If you think I'm eating anything off such

a filthy old cloth, you've got another think coming!" she said sternly. She snatched the tablecloth, took it into the kitchen, washed it in the sink and hung it out to dry. When she was satisfied with it, Rabbit put the cloth on the kitchen table and said, "Tablecloth, spread!"

Nothing happened. Rabbit scratched his head, and lifted the edge of the cloth to see if the food had come out underneath. "I don't understand it," he muttered. "It worked before."

"That crafty wind has put one over on you," said Mrs Rabbit. "You've lost all those fruit and vegetables, and all you've got to show for it is a tacky tablecloth!"

Rabbit hated it when anyone got the better of him, and he spent the whole day in a sulk.

Next morning, when the wind breezed along Shady Lane, he found Rabbit waiting for him with the tablecloth.

"I want another word with you, Wind!" Rabbit said. "You told me this tablecloth was magic — well, it's not!"

The wind made the cloth flutter. "You washed away all the magic," he said. "You should have left it as it was."

"I wasn't to know that," said Rabbit. "I know my rights, and I demand more compensation."

Now the wind knew that Rabbit was just being greedy — all the vegetables he'd eaten the previous day more than made up for the ones that were spoiled in his garden. But the wind hated any sort of argument, so he sighed and said, "All right. Here you are."

There was a whistling sound, and a battered cooking pot fell at Rabbit's feet — CLONK!

"What's this old junk?" Rabbit asked.

"A magic cooking pot," said the wind.
"Say — *Pot, pour!* — and see what happens."

So Rabbit said, "Pot, pour!" and at once the pot produced a pile of food. There were peas and beans the size of hens' eggs, and sticks of celery that were longer than walrus tusks.

With a greedy shout, Rabbit leapt on the vegetables and ate right through them, until his stomach felt tighter than a balloon filled with water.

The wind left Shady Lane, and Rabbit carried the pot indoors to show his wife.

"You mean you actually ate food from a disgusting cooking pot like that?" Mrs Rabbit gasped. "It's a wonder it didn't give you the collywobbles! Hand it over, I'm going to give it a good clean."

She took the pot into the kitchen and scrubbed it with a wire brush until its inside gleamed like silver.

But when Rabbit set the pot on the kitchen table and said, "Pot, pour!" nothing happened.

"You must have cleaned the magic away," Rabbit complained. "We should have left it just the way it was."

"That good for nothing wind has tricked us again!" said Mrs Rabbit. "He's probably laughing at you behind your back."

"We'll soon see about that!" Rabbit said grumpily.

Next morning, when the wind blew up Shady Lane, Rabbit was ready for him.

"This pot doesn't work any more!" Rabbit shouted. "My wife gave it a clean, and it's useless. I demand that you give me something that works properly!"

The wind had been busy pushing storm clouds around during the night, and he wasn't in a good mood. "You're just being greedy!" he said.

"I know my rights!" said Rabbit. "Give me something else, or I'll tell everyone how sneaky and mean you are!"

There was a roaring sound, and a big stick dropped at Rabbit's feet.

"Say — *Stick, swish!* — and see what happens," said the Wind.

Rabbit chuckled with glee as he thought about all the delicious food he was going to eat. "Stick, swish!" he said loudly.

Instantly, the stick sprang up, and began to give Rabbit a hearty whacking.

"Ooh! Ow! Call it off!" shrieked Rabbit.

"Only if you promise to leave me alone, and to stop being so greedy," said the wind.

"I promise!" Rabbit whimpered.

The wind whisked away the stick and the pot, and left Rabbit standing alone in the lane.

After that, Rabbit was a changed animal. He learned to keep his temper, and to take his fair share instead of grabbing everything he could get. He worked hard to put his garden right, and when the harvest came he gathered a bumper crop.

And the food Rabbit had grown himself tasted far better than anything he's got from the magic tablecloth and cooking pot.

# 4

# The Cow Who Flew

Most of you will have heard the story of Jack, who sold his cow to a strange old man for five magic beans. As you know, the beans grew into a beanstalk that reached right up into the clouds, and when Jack climbed it, he got into a bit of bother with an ogre. But what the story doesn't say, is what happened to Jack's cow - and it's high time the truth was told.

It was like this.

Right from the start, Cow had been suspicious of the strange old man who stopped Jack in a wood and offered him the magic beans. "I think there's something peculiar going on here," Cow said to herself, as the old man led her away. For instead of following the path that went out of the trees and into the sunshine, the old man took the path that wound deeper and deeper into the shadows. The air turned cool, and was filled with the croaking of frogs. Toadstools grew in clumps at the edge of the path and they glowed in the dimness.

"I'm not sure I like the look of this," Cow said to herself.

The further they went into the wood, the stranger the strange old man became. He took off his hat, and Cow saw that his ears were long and pointed. Then he took off his coat, and Cow saw his spindly arms and legs, and his knees that were knobblier than two bags of walnuts.

"Well, if he isn't a wood goblin, I'll eat my horns!" said Cow.

The goblin laughed nastily. "Tee hee!" he cried. "Just think — a cow for five beans! That lad Jack was even more stupid than he looked. Now I'll have milk and cream, and butter and cheese whenever I want!"

"That's what you think!" murmured Cow. "My old Ma told me to keep well clear of goblins."

The goblin lived right in the middle of the wood. He had cleared away some trees and built himself a shack. Next to the shack was a small patch of grass, and next to that were the Goblin's beans.

The goblin tethered Cow to a post set in the grass. "There you are," he said. "Eat all the grass you want, but don't touch my beans. My old Ma told me never to mix milk with magic." And he left Cow there, all day and all night.

Now Cow was used to spending the night in a cosy barn. She didn't like being out in the open with just the moon and stars for company, so when the sun rose, Cow was in a humpty, grumpy sort of mood.

The goblin came out of his shack with a three-legged stool, a wooden pail and a grin that showed all his crooked teeth. "Now for some lovely creamy milk!" he gloated.

"That's what you think!" muttered Cow.

The goblin put his pail underneath Cow, sat on the stool and tried to milk her. He teased and squeezed and tickled and tugged until his whiskers turned blue, but he didn't get a single drop of milk from Cow.

Up sprang the goblin, as angry as a stinging wasp. "That rotten, no-good Jack has swindled me!" he roared. He fixed Cow with a stare that was sourer than lemon juice. "You've got one more chance!" he said. "You give me plenty of milk this evening, or else!" And with that he stamped his foot so hard that the walls of his shack shook.

"Oh dear!" said Cow. "My old Ma was quite right — goblins are a bad lot!"

All day long, Cow chewed grass and thought milky thoughts. But the grass was poor stuff and dry as old pillows.

At sundown, the goblin came out of his shack with his stool and pail. He teased and squeezed, and tickled and tugged until his whiskers turned green, but he didn't get a single drop of milk from Cow, and he flew into a terrible rage. "This is your last chance!" he screeched. "If you don't give me a pailful of milk tomorrow morning, I'm going to slice you into steaks, grind you into mince and boil up the leftovers to make stew!" And he stamped his foot so hard that his shack nearly fell down.

Cow trembled with fear. She didn't like the idea of being sliced, ground and boiled. "Whatever can I do?" she whimpered. "I can't make milk from dry grass! I must eat something green and juicy."

Just then, the moon came up, and its light shone down on the plump, luscious beans in the goblin's garden.

"I've got to eat some!" said Cow. "Magic or not, they're my only chance!"

Cow took the tether in her mouth and pulled until it snapped. Then she walked over to the garden and started to munch as quietly as she could. "My goodness, these beans taste grand!" said Cow. "I think I'll eat them all."

But before she could finish the beans, their magic began to work. Cow felt most peculiar, and her back tingled and itched. She turned her head to try and scratch her back with one of her horns, and mooed in amazement. She had grown a pair of enormous wings, with feathers as white and soft as a snowy owl's.

"Goodness me, whatever next?" said Cow. "I'll just give them a quick shake to see if that stops the itching."

The white wings sighed as they flapped, and Cow felt herself rise into the air. With every wing sigh she rose higher, until the goblin's shack was no more than a dot on the ground far below.

Cow soared and swooped, laughing out loud. "I haven't had so much fun since I was a calf!" she declared. She flew low, so that her hooves brushed the tree tops, then flew high, so she could feel the moonlight glistening on her wings.

But as the night wore on, the magic of the beans wore off. Slowly, Cow's wings started to shrink, until they were too small to lift her. She landed near a cottage, not far from a hidden valley. Tired out by all her flying, Cow fell fast asleep and the last of the magic turned into a sweet dream.

When the goblin went out of his shack the next morning and found that Cow had

 escaped, he lost his temper good and proper. He stamped his foot so hard that the ground cracked open and swallowed him up.

As for Cow, well, of course she had landed near the cottage where Donkey, Cat, Dog and Cockerel lived and they made her so welcome that she decided to stay. She moved into the old dairy in Boggart Hollow, where she remained in comfort for the rest of her days.

And she never had anything to do with goblins ever again.

# 5

# Fox, the Crow
# and the Witch

There was a pretty little cottage at the end of Forest Road, and Fox lived there. He was a handsome chap. His coat was as red as autumn leaves, and his paws were black and silky. He had a fine bushy tail with a creamy tip, and his eyes were brighter than two marbles shining in the moonlight.

Fox was as crafty as he was handsome. He earned his living by using his wits, and they were as sharp as a sackful of new pins. In fact, he was so sly that all the other animals said, "If you shake paws with Fox, be sure to count your claws afterwards."

One sunny morning, Fox was strolling in the woods when he saw a crow, perched on a high branch in a tree. The crow had a big lump of cheese in its beak, and as soon as he saw it, Fox licked his lips. There was nothing he liked better than a nice piece of cheese, so he sat down at the foot of the tree and smiled his most charming smile. "My goodness, what a ravishing creature!" he said, in a voice as smooth as moss. "What glossy feathers you have, and your eyes sparkle like the evening stars!"

The crow wasn't used to flattery, and when she heard Fox's words, she fluffed up her feathers to show them off.

"Your voice must be as beautiful as your tail!" said Fox. "Sing me a song, and make my day!"

The crow opened her beak to caw, and the cheese dropped straight into Fox's

gaping mouth. Three
snaps of his
jaws, and it
was gone.

"Yes, you're a fine figure of a crow and
no mistake!" said Fox. "What a shame that
you're so stupid!" And he trotted off home,
chuckling to himself.

Now it so happened that the crow was
friendly with a witch, Gertie Grubshoe. As
soon as Fox had swallowed the cheese, the
angry crow flew off to Gertie's hovel on
Mount Crushmore, and told her witchy
friend all about it.

"Why, the cheeky little slyboots!" cried
Gertie. "I can see I'm going to have to
teach Fox a lesson!" And with that she

hopped on to her broomstick and swished up into the sky.

Fox was in his parlour, just about to tuck into a juicy pie that he'd swiped from the baker's shop, when there was a loud banging on his door.

"Come out at once, you red rascal!" screeched an ugly voice. "I want a word with you!"

Fox stood up, opened the door and saw Gertie Grubshoe in his front garden. "What can I do for you, lovely lady?" said Fox.

Gertie Grubshoe wasn't taken in by Fox's sweet words. She was ugly enough to make a clock strike thirteen, and she knew it.

"You stole a piece of cheese from my friend Crow this morning, and now you'll have to pay for it!" she said. "I'm going to turn you into a slug. Which would you rather be, a grey one with black spots, or a brown one with orange stripes?"

"You can't really turn me into a slug, can you?" said Fox.

"Of course I can!" snapped Gertie Grubshoe. "I'm a witch! I can turn anybody into anything!"

"I bet you can't turn yourself into something big — like an elephant," said Fox.

"An elephant?" Gertie Grubshoe said scornfully. "Easy peasy! Just watch this!"

She waved her crooked fingers in the air, and her nose grew so long that it touched the ground. Then her ears grew as big as sails, and in no time at all the witch was the most enormous elephant.

"Bravo!" cried Fox, clapping his paws

together. "But I bet you can't turn yourself into something small, like a vole!"

"Nothing simpler!" Gertie Grubshoe trumpeted.

The elephant started to shrink like a melting ice cube. It got smaller and smaller, and as it did, its trunk became a tiny snout with shivery whiskers. Its great plodding feet turned into skinny pink paws. "There you are!" squeaked Gertie Grubshoe.

"And there *you* are!" said Fox. He jumped on to the vole, and in three snaps of his jaws, it was gone. "Phew! That was a lucky escape!" Fox said, feeling pleased with himself for being so clever.

But Fox didn't feel so clever later. He had such a bad stomach ache that he didn't sleep a wink all night. "Serves me right!" he told himself. "I should have known better than to eat a witch between meals."

And he never did it again.

# 6

# Slow and Steady

Just down the road from Fox, two cottages stood side by side. Tortoise and his family lived in one cottage, and Hare lived in the other.

Hare was a busy, boastful animal. He never walked anywhere, he always ran as fast as he could, dashing about the place like a bustling breeze. Other animals stopped to look at the flowers in spring, or the beautiful autumn leaves, but Hare didn't. One quick glance and — zip! — he was off again, leaving a trail of dust behind him. Hare didn't pay much attention to anybody but himself.

Tortoise was just the opposite. He went everywhere at a slow, steady plod, and nothing could hurry him. It took him all morning to go down to the village shops and back because he thought carefully about every step. He thought when he ate, too, and spent ages chewing before swallowing food down his long, crinkled neck.

One day, Tortoise was working in the garden with his wife and two sons when Hare popped his head over the garden fence and sniggered. "I don't know how you manage to get anything done, working at that speed, Tortoise!" he said.

"Slow and steady, that's the way," Tortoise replied.

"Foo!" snorted Hare. "Why, I could do the washing, dust the house, clean the windows and polish all my bits and bobs in the time it takes you to weed your lettuce patch."

"Well, that's where I'm different from you, Hare," said Tortoise. "You like to fuss and flit, and leave things half done. I've got staying power. I stick at one thing until it's finished."

Hare was very quick-tempered, and what Tortoise said offended him. "My way of doing things is much better than yours!" he snapped.

"It's not better — just different," said Tortoise.

"It's better, and I'll prove it to you!" Hare said. "Tomorrow morning, we'll have a race up to the spring at the top of the valley.

Let's see who gets home first with a pail of fresh water. It's bound to be me!"

Now Tortoise's temper was slower than a river of treacle, but by now Hare had got it going. Tortoise's dander was up, and no mistake. "All right, Hare," he said. "I'll meet you outside your garden gate at eight o' clock sharp, and may the best animal win."

Hare gave a sneering laugh, and darted off.

Tortoise's wife came lumbering up to him. "You reckless reptile!" she scolded. "You've been too hasty for your own good. Hare is going to beat you, and we'll never hear the end of his boasting!"

"I'm not so sure," chuckled Tortoise. "Hare is good at running, but he's not so good at thinking. I've got a plan!"

That night, Tortoise explained the plan to his family. Then he and his sons picked up pails and set off up the valley by the light of the moon. A third of the way along the path to the spring was a holly bush.

"You hide under there until Hare comes along," Tortoise told his eldest son. "Then step out and say what I told you to say."

"Right you are!" said Tortoise's son.

Two thirds of the way up the path to the spring was a tall oak tree.

"You hide behind the trunk until Hare comes along," Tortoise told his youngest son. "Then step out and say what I told you to say."

"Right you are!" the son said.

Tortoise carried on up the path until he reached the spring. The sun had begun to

rise by the time he got there. He filled his
pail with water, then settled down for a
doze.

At eight o' clock, Hare hopped over his
garden fence. Tortoise's wife was waiting
for him, but Hare didn't notice who she
was. He was in such a rush that he thought
it was Tortoise himself. "Are you ready?"
Hare said. "I'll give you a start, if you like."

"Slow and steady does it," said Tortoise's
wife.

"One . . . two . . . three . . . GO!" shouted
Hare, and he was off. He ran so fast that
his long ears bent backwards, and his
whiskers hummed in the wind.

A third of the way
along the path, Hare
stopped to look back.
Tortoise was nowhere
in sight. "Yoo-hoo!"
called Hare. "Tortoise, where are you?"

"Right here," said a voice.
"Slow and steady does it."
Tortoise's son crept out
from under the holly bush,
holding his pail in his mouth.
Hare was so astonished, he thought it
was Tortoise. "You can run faster than I
thought!" he gasped. "But you
won't catch me now!"

Hare raced off up
the path. He ran
so fast that his
shadow had to
stretch out long
and thin to keep up with him.

Two thirds of the way up the path, Hare stopped to look behind him. Tortoise was nowhere to be seen. Then, suddenly, Hare heard a voice saying, "Here I am, Hare! Slow and steady does it," and Tortoise's youngest son appeared from behind the oak tree.

"Well, roll me over in the clover and pickle my paws in plum juice!" cried Hare. "I can see I'm going to have to run my fastest!"

Hare sped along the path. He ran so fast that he left his breath behind, and when he reached the spring he fell down until it caught up with him.

"What kept you?" said a voice.

Hare looked around and saw that Tortoise was waiting for him.

"How did you get here so quickly?" Hare panted.

"I wasn't quick at all," Tortoise told him. "Slow and steady does it. Are you ready to race home?"

"I must have a rest first!" Hare groaned. "I'm worn out. You carry on."

So Tortoise started down the path with his pail of water. Hare was so tired that he fell asleep, and he didn't wake up until the stars were out. His legs ached and his paws were sore. He limped back to his cottage, feeling sorry for himself. When he got to his garden gate, he found Tortoise there.

"I can't understand how you beat me," said Hare. "I was certain that I was going to win."

"I told you, I've got staying power!" Tortoise declared.

After that, Hare calmed down a bit. He stopped boasting about how fast he was, and he took his time over things. In fact, he slowed down long enough to find himself a wife and raise a family. When his children grew, and started dashing all over the place, Hare said to them, "Take your time! Slow and steady does it."

And every time Tortoise heard this, he laughed until his shell echoed.

# 7

# Fox's Revenge

Wolf lived alone in a house on Shady Lane. He was long and lean, and his fur was as grey as smoke. His green eyes seemed to burn, and he had a wide, hungry smile. On nights when the moon was full, Wolf went out into his garden to howl, and the sound made the whole of Boggart Hollow shiver. Wolf would have been a fearsome beast indeed, if it hadn't been for his tail. It was as bald as a pebble.

When Wolf walked down the street, the other animals nodded to him respectfully, but after he passed by, they turned to look at his bald pink tail and they giggled. "I wonder where his fur went?" they asked each other, but no one seemed to know.

This is how it happened..

One fine, frosty winter's morning, Wolf went out for a slink down Shady Lane. He hadn't gone far when he met Fox coming the other way. Fox was carrying a pie that he'd filched from a kitchen windowsill. The pie was still warm, and it steamed in the cold air. It smelled so delicious that Wolf's stomach began to gurgle.

"Good morning, Fox!" said Wolf, gazing at the pie with his great green eyes.

"G-good morning," Fox said nervously, staring at Wolf's long fangs.

"That's a fine-looking pie," said Wolf. "I wonder if it tastes as good as it looks?"

"Why not try some and find out?" said Fox. He broke off a small piece of the pie and gave it to Wolf.

Wolf chewed and swallowed, and licked

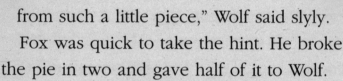

his whiskers.
"How does
it taste?"
asked Fox.
"Hard to tell
from such a little piece," Wolf said slyly.

Fox was quick to take the hint. He broke the pie in two and gave half of it to Wolf.

"Hmm!" said Wolf, talking with his mouth full. "I still can't seem to make up my mind. Perhaps I should have another taste, just to make sure."

With a heavy sigh, Fox handed over the rest of the pie and watched sulkily as it disappeared down Wolf's greedy throat.

"It was as good as it looked after all," said Wolf, as he licked the last few crumbs from the tip of his nose. "A very fine pie indeed!" He walked off, laughing to himself at the way he had got the better of Fox.

Fox was furious. "No one tricks me and

gets away with it!" he growled quietly. "I'll show you a thing or two about cunning, you big bully!"

A few nights later, Wolf was dozing in an armchair by the fire when a knock came at his door. It was Fox, wearing a smile that was as slippery as satin. "My dear fellow!" Fox exclaimed. "I was just passing, and I wondered if you would care to join me. The duck pond has frozen over, and there's a splendid view of the full moon from the middle of it. We can look at the moon together and you can howl while I yap."

"What a kind thought!" said Wolf. "I haven't had a good howl in ages."

Fox and Wolf strolled to the duck pond, and when he reached

the edge, Fox sniffed. "I smell cheese!" he said.

"I can't," said Wolf.

"I know cheese when I smell it, and I smell it now," Fox insisted. He took two steps on to the frozen pond and barked, "Look!"

There, in the middle of the pond, was the moon's reflection, as round and yellow as a Cheddar cheese. Wolf ran over and tried to take a bite, but he bumped his nose against the cold, hard ice. "Ow!" he yelped. "It's frozen into the ice. How can we get at it?"

Fox walked round the reflection, pretending to think hard. "I'll run back to my cottage for an axe," he said at last. "We'll chop out that cheese in no time. You stay here, and cover the cheese with your tail so that no one else finds it."

"Good thinking!" said Wolf. He sat on the ice and spread out his tail.

Fox hurried off towards his cottage, but as soon as he was out of sight round a corner, he sneaked back and hid behind a tree so that he could watch Wolf.

It grew colder and colder. Wolf's bottom got number and number, until he couldn't feel it at all. "Where has Fox got to?" he grumbled. "It feels as if I've been waiting here for hours!"

Just then, Fox called out, "Hunters are coming! Hunters are coming!"

Wolf panicked. He tried to run away, but something held him back, and his claws screeched on the ice. He turned his head and saw that his tail had stuck to the surface of the pond.

"Hunters are coming!" Fox shouted again.

Wolf heaved with all his strength. There was a ripping sound, and suddenly he was free. He ran straight home and shut all his doors and windows. Only when he turned the last lock did he notice how peculiar his tail felt. He tried to swish it, but it only wiggled. Wolf glanced over his shoulder and saw that he had left all the fur from his tail stuck to the ice on the pond.

Wolf never found out that Fox had tricked him. Indeed, he was terribly grateful to Fox, and when they next met, Wolf shook Fox by the paw. "If it hadn't been for you, Fox, those hunters might have caught me!" Wolf said.

"Yes, but it's a shame about your tail," said Fox.

"I know," Wolf agreed sadly. "But it's better to lose the hair from your tail than lose your life."

"Fur better!" said Fox, and his eyes twinkled like frosty stars.

# 8

# Diddy Goat, Middy Goat and Great Goat

Half way along Spring Lane stood a cottage with white walls and a thatched roof, and the three goat brothers lived there. The youngest was Diddy Goat. He was only little, but his mind was as fast as a flea. When he walked along, he liked to hop and frisk and he was happier than a cow in clover.

The second brother was called Middy Goat. He was bigger than Diddy, but not quite so sharp witted. He walked at a steady trot, because he was always thinking about something, and it was usually something gloomy.

The third brother was the oldest, and the biggest of the lot. His name was Great Goat and when he walked, the ground shook. Great Goat was so strong and had such a bad temper that the other animals in the village were always careful to speak to him politely. They called him Mr Goat and kept a watchful eye on his long, curved horns.

Throughout most of the year, the goat brothers grazed on the lush grass that grew on the hills above the valley. In winter, when the fields were covered with snow, the goats stayed in their cottage and ate hay, with a bit of moss every now and then to make a change.

After a few months, the brothers grew heartily sick of hay. They couldn't even stand the sight of the stuff, so they ate with their eyes closed.

At breakfast one morning, Diddy Goat heaved a heavy sigh and said, "Just think, spring will soon be here, and the fields will be full of fresh grass!"

"Don't be so sure," said Middy Goat. "I think the weather's going to take a turn for the worse. It'll be weeks and weeks before the spring comes."

When he heard his brother's words, Great Goat jumped up from his place at the table. "I can't stand it any longer!" he roared. "I'm off out!"

"Where are you going?" asked Diddy Goat.

"To have a word with winter about the weather," said Great Goat, his voice growling like thunder.

Great Goat charged outside and turned his head this way and that. "Where are you, winter?" he bellowed. "Stand up and fight!" He charged down the road, shaking his

head so that his horns butted the wind.
"Take that, you big coward!" he shouted.

Even winter couldn't stand the sight of
Great Goat in a rage, and all at once the
sky cleared. The sun came out, flowers
opened and the birds began to sing.

"That's more like it," Great Goat said to
the sky. "And mind you keep it this way!"

In a few days, the snow had melted and
the hills were green. The goat brothers left
their cottage, crossed a wooden  bridge
that stood over a river, and climbed the hill
to the place where the grass was sweetest.
They spent the whole morning eating, until

at last Diddy Goat could eat no more. "I'm full!" he told his brothers. "I'm going home for a snooze," and he frisked off down the hillside towards the bridge.

Now the goat brothers didn't know, but on the coldest, darkest night of winter, a troll had come down from his icy cave on Mount Crushmore, looking for a cosy spot to sleep until spring. The troll had found a hole under the bridge and curled up inside it. The spring sunshine had warmed him until he woke up. He opened his bleary, bloodshot eyes, and smacked his lips. "By my thumbs and elbows, I'm starving!" he said to himself. "I'm so hungry, I could eat a horse between two soggy mattresses! I wonder what there is in the way of grub round these parts?"

Just then, Diddy Goat stepped on to the bridge, and the troll heard the clatter of little hooves on the planks. "Aye, aye! That sounds like lunch!" chuckled the troll, and he hopped up on to the bridge as niftily as if he had springs inside his boots.

When Diddy Goat saw the troll's big teeth and hungry eyes, he began to tremble. "G-good day, Mr Troll," he bleated.

"It's a good day for me, but not for you, feller-me-lad," said the troll. "I must have me grub, and you're it, so it's into my cooking pot with you."

Straight away, Diddy Goat's clever brain went to work and he started laughing.

"What's so funny?" the troll asked.

"The thought of you eating me," Diddy Goat explained. "Why, there's nothing to me but hair and bones. If you wait a while, my big brother will come along. He'll make a much better meal than I would."

"Hmm," said the troll, rubbing his chin. "You are a bit on the titchy side, now you come to mention it. Off with you, before I change my mind."

And Diddy Goat frisked safely home.

Not long after, Middy Goat felt full, and decided to go back to the cottage. "I shouldn't have eaten so much," he grumbled as he trotted along. "I'm sure to have nightmares when I go to sleep!"

Middy Goat was so busy being miserable that he didn't notice the Troll until he almost bumped into him.

"Ah!" said the troll, with a ghastly grin. "I've been expecting you. The little goat said his big brother would be along soon, and here you are. I think I'll build a fire and roast you over it."

"Oh dear!" said Middy Goat. "I knew something awful would happen today. It's all a dreadful mistake!" and he burst into tears.

"Mistake, what mistake?" said the troll, frowning.

"Well, when Diddy said his big brother was coming, he didn't mean me," Middy Goat said. "I know I'm bigger than he is, but I'm nowhere near as big as our biggest brother. He's enormous!"

A greedy gleam came into the troll's eyes. "Is that a fact?" he rumbled.

"He'll be along at any minute," said Middy Goat. "And anyway, if you ate me, I'm sure you wouldn't enjoy it. I'm bound to taste awful, and you'll get a terrible stomach ache. I can't do anything right, you see — not even being food."

By now, Middy Goat was sobbing so pitifully that the troll's stony heart softened.

"Be off with you!" sniffled the troll. "I'll wait here for your brother. Go home, and try to be a bit more positive about yourself."

So Middy Goat trotted home, with tears trickling into his beard.

The troll sat down in the middle of the bridge and waited until the shadows grew long as the sun went down. Then he heard a rumbling noise. "That must be my stomach!" he said.

But it wasn't, it was the sound of Great Goat coming down the hillside. When Great Goat reached the far end of the bridge and saw the troll, he scuffed the ground with his hooves, throwing up big chunks of earth.

"Oh, my knees and nostrils!" cried the troll. "You'll take a week to get through! You're a big feller, aren't you?"

"Big?" growled Great Goat. "What do you mean, big? Are you trying to tell me that there's something wrong with being BIG?"

Great Goat was so angry, hot breath came down his nose like the steam from two boiling kettles. He lowered his head and charged like an express train.

The wooden bridge rocked beneath his pounding hooves, and when he reached the troll, Great Goat caught him on his horns and tossed him into the air.

Up and up went the troll, spinning like a cartwheel. He went so high that he bumped his head against a cloud, and it rained over him until he was soaked. Then he fell down and down, and landed in the ocean with a mighty splash. "If there's one thing I hate, it's food that fights back!" he said to himself as he swam towards the shore.

And from that time on Troll ate nothing but fruit and vegetables.

# 9

# The Boggart Hollow Tug-of-War

Of course, Great Goat wasn't the only strong animal in the village. Horse and Ox lived at Number Seven, High Street, and Squirrel was their next door neighbour. Squirrel got on well enough with Horse and Ox, but they didn't get on with each other. Though they were the best of friends, they argued from daybreak to sundown — and sometimes all night as well. The argument was about who was the strongest beast in Boggart Hollow.

"It has to be me!" Horse said. "When I

used to work on a farm, I could pull a wagon with so much hay in it that it took seven men all day to unload it."

"Only as much as that?" said Ox. "When I worked on a farm, I used to pull the cart to market. I once carried a load of potatoes that was so big, it took ten people a week to peel them all."

"I don't believe it!" whinnied Horse. "You're nowhere near as strong as I am. Just take a look at my muscles!"

"Ha! I've seen acorns bigger than that!" Ox bellowed.

And so they went on for hours at an end.

All day long, poor Squirrel had to listen to the sound of Horse and Ox shouting at each other, and if they argued at night, she didn't have a wink of sleep.

One day, Squirrel went into the forest for some peace and quiet. She was searching for a comfy spot to take a snooze when she came to a clearing. In the middle of the clearing was a patch of brambles nearly as tall as a house. A tunnel ran through the brambles, just big enough for Squirrel to squeeze through, and as soon as she saw it, it gave her an idea. She hurried home and got there just in time to see Horse stepping out through his front door.

"Good morning, Horse," Squirrel said brightly. "Where's Ox?"

"Working in the garden," Horse said sulkily. "We're not speaking at the moment. We had a row last night, because he said he was the strongest beast in Boggart Hollow, when everybody knows that I am."

"Well, you're both wrong," Squirrel declared. "Because the strongest beast in Boggart Hollow is me."

"You?" gasped Horse. "You're so scrawny that if I breathed out hard it would blow you away!"

"I'm dainty, but I'm powerful," Squirrel said. "I could pull as hard as you in a tug-of-war any day of the week."

Horse was so tickled that he began to laugh.

"I'll prove it," Squirrel said. "Meet me at six o' clock on the east side of the big bramble patch in the forest, and bring a piece of strong rope with you."

Squirrel left Horse chuckling away, and went into her garden. Over the fence she could see Ox, digging up turnips with his horns.

"Good morning, Ox," said Squirrel. "How are you and your friend Horse today?"

"Horse is no friend of mine," Ox replied. "We were arguing all night. He just won't admit that I'm the strongest beast in

Boggart Hollow."

"That's because you're not," Squirrel said cheekily.

Ox was so angry that when he flicked his tail, it cracked like a whip. "What?" he cried. "So, you think Horse is stronger than I am, do you?"

"No," said Squirrel. "I'm as strong as the pair of you put together."

"You?" grunted Ox. "You're so feeble, you couldn't snap a spider's thread!"

"Looks can be deceiving," said Squirrel. "If I took you on in a tug-of-war, you couldn't shift me an inch."

Ox thought that this was so funny, he lowed and laughed at the same time and gave himself hiccups.

"If you don't believe me, meet me on the west side of the big bramble patch in the forest at six o' clock," said Squirrel. "And bring a piece of strong rope with you."

"Are you sure a bit of cotton wouldn't do?" Ox sneered.

"It has to be rope," Squirrel insisted. "The thicker the better!"

Horse and Ox spent the day avoiding each other, and Squirrel spent the afternoon in bed, catching up on her sleep. At five o'clock, she woke up and went off to the bramble patch. Once there, she squeezed inside the tunnel and waited.

Just before six o' clock, Squirrel heard the clopping of Horse's hooves approaching from the east.

She peered through the brambles, and saw that Horse had a rope tied around his neck. He was carrying the loose end in his mouth.

"Throw the rope to me," said Squirrel. "Then wait until I say pull."

"Wouldn't you rather be in the open?" asked Horse. "When I pull you through the brambles, the thorns will scratch you into shreds."

"I know what I'm doing!" Squirrel said.

Horse threw the rope to her, and Squirrel laid it on the ground. As she did, she heard the slow thud of Ox's hooves approaching from the west. Like Horse, Ox had a rope around his neck.

"Throw the rope to me, and wait until I say pull," Squirrel said.

"Come out of there!" said Ox. "When I drag you through those brambles, you'll be scratched into strips."

"I know what I'm doing!" Squirrel snapped.

Ox threw the rope into the tunnel, and Squirrel caught hold of it. Then she tied Ox's rope to Horse's, and shouted, "Pull!"

Horse took a step, and so did Ox, and the rope went tight.

Horse heaved and huffed with all his might, while Ox pulled and puffed. They pulled with all their strength, but neither could shift the other.

After half an hour of sweating and straining, both animals fell exhausted to the ground. Squirrel untied their ropes, then popped out of the brambles to talk to Horse. "Well?" she said.

"You're right!" Horse admitted breathlessly. "I gave it all I've got, but it wasn't enough to beat you!" Horse's bottom lip wobbled nervously. "Er . . . you won't tell anyone else about this, will you?" he said.

"As long as you stop arguing with Ox about who is the strongest animal in the village," said Squirrel.

"Agreed!" said Horse. Wearily, he picked

himself up off the floor and staggered home.

When he was safely out of sight, Squirrel dashed through the tunnel to speak to Ox. "Had enough?" she said.

"I haven't got a puff left in me!" Ox panted. "You're much stronger than you look." Ox rolled his eyes anxiously. "Er . . . you won't tell anyone about our little match, will you?" he said.

"Only if you don't carry on arguing with Horse," Squirrel told him.

"There's nothing left to argue about," said Ox. "You're the strongest beast in Boggart Hollow, no contest!"

And from that day onwards, there was peace between Horse and Ox. Each was too ashamed to tell the other about playing tug-of-war with Squirrel, and they never quarrelled again.

# 10

# Hedgehog's Love

Across the road from the Goat Brothers'
house stood the tiny cottage where
Hedgehog lived with his granny. Hedgehog
was extremely short sighted and was always
bumping into things. He sometimes thought
that he was talking to Wolf when he was
talking to Fox, and got Dog mixed up with
Cat, which was most embarrassing. As a
result, Hedgehog became rather shy and
didn't say much to anyone.

Though Hedgehog was small and prickly,
he had a big soft heart and yearned to
meet the lady hedgehog of his dreams. He
spent days moping about the cottage,

sighing loudly.

Granny, who was old and quite wise, knew just what was wrong. "Don't you worry, my dear," she told her grandson. "One day a fine young lady hedgehog will come along, and you'll sweep her off her feet."

"I don't think so!" Hedgehog said sadly. "Lady hedgehogs never visit Boggart Hollow. I'm doomed to be a bachelor all my days!"

"Love will always find a way," said Granny. "You mark my words."

One warm summer night, loneliness made Hedgehog's heart ache so badly that he couldn't get to sleep, and he decided to go for a walk in the forest. The moon was up, and to Hedgehog's blurry eyes it seemed that all the trees and ferns were shining through a silvery mist.

"What a perfect night!" Hedgehog murmured, and the thought that there was no one to share it with him plunged him into a deep gloom. He wandered about, not really going anywhere, and he came to a spot where he'd never been before - a tumbledown cottage on the edge of a forest glade. Hedgehog rambled over towards the ruin, and suddenly he stopped still, quivering with excitement. For there in the doorway, he could just make out a small, prickly shape.

"It's . . . HER!" gasped Hedgehog. "The lady of my dreams!"

Too shy to move any closer, Hedgehog cleared his throat and said, "Isn't the moonlight lovely?"

There was no reply, so Hedgehog said, "Um, do you live far from here?"

No answer came.

"Oh dear!" thought Hedgehog. "She must be even shyer than I am. I'd better leave her alone before she runs away."

"So nice to meet you," he said aloud. "If you pass this way tomorrow night, perhaps we'll meet again."

And he hurried home with a singing heart.

Next morning, Hedgehog told his granny what had happened.

"You must go again tonight," said Granny. "If she comes back, you'll know that she's taken a shine to you, and you must woo her."

"How?" cried Hedgehog.

"Just tell her what's in your heart," Granny said. "If she's the one for you, she'll understand what you mean."

Hedgehog thought about this for a long time, and the more he thought the less happy he became. "I don't know how to turn my heart into words," he thought. "I'll go and see Mayor Donkey. I'm sure he'll give me some advice."

And he scampered off to Donkey's cottage.

Donkey listened carefully to what Hedgehog had to say, then said, "You must take a present that shows how you feel."

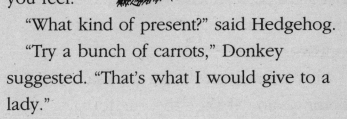

"What kind of present?" said Hedgehog.

"Try a bunch of carrots," Donkey suggested. "That's what I would give to a lady."

So Hedgehog went straight home and

pulled up the six longest, fattest carrots in
his garden. He washed all the earth off
them, tied them into a bunch, and that
night he carried the bunch to the ruin in
the forest. When he got there, he saw the
small, bristly shape waiting for him in the
doorway.

"I brought you these carrots," Hedgehog
said. "I do hope you like them."

Just as on the night before, there was no
reply, and after a few minutes of silence,
Hedgehog's shyness got the better of him.
He dropped the carrots on the ground,
scuttled home and went straight to bed.

When he woke next morning,
Hedgehog's heartache was worse than ever.
"She won't talk to me!" he grumbled to
Granny.

"Then you must do the talking for you
both," Granny said.

This advice only made Hedgehog fret. "I

must go and see Fox," he thought. "He's the cleverest beast in Boggart Hollow. He'll know what to do."

So Hedgehog went to Fox's home, and when he had made quite sure that it *was* Fox, and not Wolf, he told him all about the ruined cottage and his bashful love.

"Carrots are no way to a lady's heart!" Fox declared. "You must speak romantic words, as smooth and sweet as honey."

"But I don't know any romantic words!" wailed Hedgehog.

"Then I'll help you," said Fox. "I'll come with you to the glade tonight. I'll hide somewhere, and tell you what to say."

This seemed such a good idea to Hedgehog that his heart fluttered like a skylark's wings.

All that day, the hours crawled by, but at last the sun went down and night fell. Hedgehog and Fox set off into the forest, and when they reached the glade, Fox hid behind a tree. Hedgehog stood in the moonlight, staring longingly at the prickly shape in the doorway of the ruin.

"Tell her that her eyes shine like the new moon!" Fox whispered.

"Um, excuse me!" said Hedgehog. "I hope you don't mind my saying so, but your eyes shine like the new moon!"

"Now tell her that her spikes are sharper than pine needles!" Fox urged.

"And your spikes are sharper than pine needles," Hedgehog repeated.

"Well?" said Fox. "What's happening?"

"Nothing," Hedgehog replied. "She hasn't moved a muscle. She hasn't even picked up the carrots I left here last night."

"She must have a heart of stone!" muttered Fox. He peered around the trunk of the tree. "Er . . . Hedgehog, dear fellow," he said quietly. "I don't think that romantic words will be of any use to you."

"She doesn't like me - I knew it!" Hedgehog groaned.

"No, it isn't that," said Fox. "It's just that my eyes are sharper than yours, and . . . well, it isn't a lady hedgehog at all."

"Isn't it?" exclaimed Hedgehog.

"No," Fox said. "I'm afraid you've fallen in love with a scrubbing brush."

Hedgehog couldn't believe his ears, but when Fox took him right up close to the ruin, he saw that it was true. What he had taken to be the love of his life was nothing but an old scrubbing brush, left behind when the cottage was deserted.

Poor Hedgehog ran home and cried so many tears into his pillow that it went soggy, and squidged when he rested his head against it.

But Granny was right, love will always find a way. A week later, another family of hedgehogs came to Boggart Hollow. They moved into a house on Forest Road, next door to Tortoise. When their pretty young daughter met Hedgehog, they fell in love at first sight.

Well, when they got close enough to see each other properly, anyway.

# 11

# The Monster in the Well

Pig lived on the High Street, a few doors down from Squirrel, Horse and Ox. Pig was highly respectable, and very particular about keeping his house clean — but he was the vainest beast in Boggart Hollow, bar none.

If Pig was strolling along the High Street, and happened to catch sight of his reflection in a window, he stopped to admire it. "My, just look at those smart pink trotters!" he would sigh. "Look at that tail, it's as curly as a corkscrew. What a fine figure of a pig!"

Because Pig thought so much of himself, he took it for granted that the other animals did too. "What a dull old place this would be without me!" Pig said to himself, as he stuck his snout in, giving advice where it wasn't wanted. If anyone tried to do anything while Pig was near, he was sure to rush over and tell them a better way of doing it. Pig was an expert on everything - or so he claimed, anyway.

So, when the annual election came around, no one was terribly surprised when Pig announced that he wanted to be Mayor instead of Donkey. He hung a big banner from his bedroom window, and on the banner it said VOTE FOR CHANGE! VOTE FOR PIG!'

On election day, a crowd of animals gathered in the village square to hear Pig and Donkey make their speeches.

Donkey went first. "My friends," he said. "You all know me, and I know all of you. You know how I do things, and if I am elected Mayor, I'll carry on in the same way. But if you would rather vote for Pig, please do. I shan't be offended, and we'll go on being good friends."

There was a ripple of applause when Donkey finished, and then Pig spoke up for himself. "My fellow citizens!" he said grandly. "Donkey has done a good job as Mayor, but I'm sure I could do an even better job. It's time for a change.

Boggart Hollow needs someone new to lead it into the future. Someone with skill, and wisdom - above all, someone with courage!"

At that moment, Pig's speech was interrupted by a scream. Everyone turned to look, and saw Mrs Rabbit racing up High Street towards them. Her fur was spiky, her whiskers were quivering, and her eyes stared wildly. "Run for your lives!" she shouted. "There's a monster in the well!"

"A monster?" said Donkey.

"I was just about to draw a pail of water from the well, when a voice said:

*Don't you dare! Don't you dare!*
*This well is mine, beware, beware!* "
said Mrs Rabbit.

"What kind of voice was it?" Pig asked.

"A great big terrible monstrous voice!" squeaked Mrs Rabbit, and she swooned away.

Great Goat was in the crowd. He scraped his hooves on the ground and snorted hot breath down his nostrils. "Let me at him!" he rumbled. "I'm not afraid of any monster! I'll give him beware, beware!" And before anyone could stop him, Great Goat went galloping off down the street.

A few minutes later he came back, with his knees knocking together. "It's t-t-true!" he stammered. "I got to the well, and I heard a great big terrible monstrous voice say:

*Don't you dare! Don't you dare!*
*This well is mine, beware, beware!*

It's fair put the wind up me, I can tell you. I'm going home for a little lie down."

The crowd muttered in a worried way. If there was a monster in the well, where would Boggart Hollow get its clean water? There was the spring at the top of the valley but it was a long, hard walk up to it.

Pig was as nervous as anyone else, but he saw a chance to impress the other animals, and he grabbed it. "Stand aside and leave this to me!" he declared. "I told you that Boggart Hollow needed someone with courage, and I'm that someone!"

"No," said Donkey. "I'm the Mayor. It's my job to deal with any trouble, so I'll go."

"We'll both go," Pig insisted, "and we'll see whose courage fails first!"

The well was at the far end of High Street, and Donkey and Pig walked towards it side by side. The other animals followed them at a safe distance.

"Feeling nervous?" Pig asked Donkey.

"Yes," Donkey admitted. "Aren't you?"

"Me?" said Pig. "I've got nerves of steel!"

As they got closer to the well, both animals noticed how strange and creepy it looked in the afternoon shadows.

"I think I'm feeling a little afraid," said Donkey. "Are you afraid, Pig?"

"Me?" said Pig. "I don't know the meaning of the word fear."

They walked right up to the well, and all at once from inside came a great big terrible monstrous voice, saying,

*"Don't you dare! Don't you dare!*
*This well is mine, beware, beware!"*

When he heard the voice,
Pig squealed. His ears
flopped down over
his eyes and his
tail went straight.
"I'd like to go
on, but I can't!"
he whimpered.
"I've, er, just remembered that I ought to be
somewhere else!" And he shot off home,
faster than a piece of elastic being twanged.

Donkey was alone. He'd never felt so
alone in his life. He wished that he could
go home too, but he knew that the whole
village was depending on him. He took a
few shaky steps forwards, and the great big
terrible monstrous voice came again.

*"Don't you dare! Don't you dare!*
*This well is mine, beware, beware!"*

"It's not your well at all!" Donkey said
boldly. "This well is public property, and

you're trespassing, so be off with you!"

"*Oh!*" said the voice. *"I'm terribly sorry. I didn't mean to be a nuisance. If you give me a hand to get out, I'll leave straight away."*

Donkey was so surprised that he forgot about being frightened. He looked down into the well, and there at the bottom was a little frog, swimming about. "Where's the monster?" Donkey cried.

*"There's no monster, just me!"* said the frog, and the deep, dark, echoey well made his voice boom like a cannon.

When Donkey realised that he'd been frightened by a frog, he burst out laughing. "I'll get you out of there," he said. "I think you'll be much happier in the duck pond!"

Donkey hauled the frog up in the well's bucket, and when the frog popped his head over the rim, all the other animals saw him and they laughed too. In fact everyone thought it was a great joke.

Everyone except Pig. He was so ashamed of making a fool of himself in front of everybody that he didn't show his face around the village for a long time afterwards.

And Donkey won the election, of course.

# 12

# A Sticky End

Magpie was a terrible thief — she'd steal
the sunshine from a summer's afternoon
and turn it into evening if she could. She
lived in the rickety spire of the old church
on the edge of the village square. It was
high in the air, but it suited Magpie down
to the ground, because she had a grand
view of Boggart Hollow, and the spire was
so rickety that no one could climb up to
reach her.

Magpie loved to steal. Bright, shiny
things were her favourite, but she wasn't
fussy — anything would do. She took the
Mayor's chain from Donkey, swooping

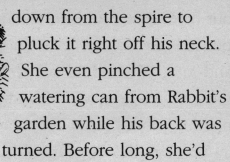

down from the spire to pluck it right off his neck. She even pinched a watering can from Rabbit's garden while his back was turned. Before long, she'd stolen from every animal in the village, and if they asked for their belongings back, she popped her head over the edge of her nest and laughed a loud, cackling laugh — "Crack-attack-attack!"

The beasts of Boggart Hollow were fed up with Magpie's thieving. They held a meeting in the village hall to see if they could come up with a way of stopping her. Donkey took charge of the meeting, but before he could say a word, Mrs Rat pushed her way to the front of the crowd and said, "We should talk to Magpie. She must be made to understand that stealing is nothing more than bad manners!"

"Quite right!" Pig agreed.

"You'll never talk to her while she stays up on that church spire," said Dog.

"What spire?" said Hedgehog, blinking his short-sighted eyes.

"I say we go to the church right now!" Great Goat rumbled. "Ox, Horse and I will knock the place down and then we can drive Magpie out of the village."

Hare and Rabbit waggled their ears in agreement, and Cockerel crowed, "That's the thing to do!"

But Wolf shook his head. "Magpie will only fly into the forest and go on stealing from there," he said.

"If I had some magic beans," said Cow, "I could fly after Magpie and make sure that she never comes back."

"But we don't have any magic beans," Cat said.

Then Tortoise spoke in his slow, thoughtful way. "Magpie has to be taught a lesson to stop her stealing once and for all," he said. "I think I know how." And Tortoise told the other animals his plan.

When Tortoise had finished, Fox turned to him and bowed. "My dear fellow, that's brilliant!" said Fox.

"Please allow me to congratulate you on your craftiness."

The animals set to work straight away. Donkey went back to his cottage to get a gold coin that had been left behind by Ned Flowers and his gang. He took it to Squirrel's house, and Squirrel polished it with her bushy tail until it gleamed.

Meanwhile, the other animals carried buckets to Pig's house. The buckets were filled with sticky stuff, and they were all poured into an old tin bath. Mud, eggs, flour, honey and pond-slime were mixed together to make a thick, gummy gloop.

An hour before sunrise, Wolf and Fox - the stealthiest animals in Boggart Hollow - crept into the village square. Fox placed the gold coin on the ground and helped Wolf to pour a big pool of the gummy gloop all around it. Then they joined the other animals who were hiding in the village hall.

As soon as the sun came up, Magpie woke. She stretched her wings, preened her feathers and looked out at the village below. At once she spotted the gold coin, gleaming like a golden spark in the square. "Crack-attack-attack!" Magpie cackled. "That's just the job for my treasure hoard!"

With a greedy glint in her eyes, Magpie flew down from the spire, hopped right into the gloop and stuck like a toffee on the bottom of a shoe. "Crack-attack!" cried Magpie.

"What's all this?" She bent her head to try and peck her claws free - and her beak stuck to the ground. "Crack-attack-attack!" wailed Magpie.

"Help! Unstick me, someone!"

The doors of the village hall flew open, and Great Goat clattered out. "I'll unstick you all right!" he said. "I'm going to butt you so high in the air that you'll come down on the other side of nowhere." He charged across the square, heading straight for Magpie.

But Great Goat had forgotten about the gloop. As soon as his hooves touched it, he was stuck. "Bosh and botheration!" he roared. "Get me out of this stuff!"

All the animals rushed over to help Great Goat, but there were so many of them that they got in one another's way. In the hustle and bustle, Donkey, Ox and Horse got stuck to Great Goat. Cockerel got stuck on Pig's back, Squirrel's tail stuck to Cat's and Rabbit, Hare and Mrs Rat got stuck to Hedgehog, which was extremely prickly and painful. Fox and Wolf got themselves into a tangle with Cow and found that they couldn't get untangled. There was a shouting, crowing, mooing, squealing, squeaking, howling rumpus that was so loud it knocked two loose slates off the church roof.

The only animal who managed to stay out of the mess was Tortoise. He took such a long time to cross the square that there was no room for anyone else to get stuck by the time he arrived. "Dear, dear, dear!" he said. "You beasts are always in such a hurry, you never stop to think."

"This is all your fault!" snapped Great Goat. "Your idea got us into this pickle.

Now think of a way to get us out of it!"

"Hmm, tricky!" Tortoise said. "Thinking won't do any good, I'm afraid. This calls for a ponder!" And he pulled his head inside his shell, where it was dark and quiet.

At noon, the hot sun began to bake the gloop, so that it gave off an awful smell.

"Mr Hedgehog!" Mrs Rat said crossly. "Please stop prickling my tail!"

"As soon as you stop tickling my nose with your whiskers!" said Hedgehog.

"Stop treading on my hoof!" Ox told Horse.

"I'm not treading!" Horse said. "Your hoof's stuck to the ground and mine's stuck on top of it."

"Oh dear!" Pig gasped. "What I wouldn't give for a long, cool drink of water!"

At this, Tortoise pushed his head out of his shell. "Water, that's it!" he exclaimed. "I'll nip down to the well for a bucketful right away!"

Tortoise took ages, but at last he returned, carrying a bucket of water in his mouth. Very carefully, he tipped it over Fox — SLOOSH! The water washed away the gloop, and Fox was free.

Fox ran to the well and brought back more water which he slooshed all over Wolf and Cow. When Wolf and Cow were unstuck, they ran to get buckets, and before long the air was filled with the sounds of scampering feet and slooshing.

Right underneath the sticky pile of

animals was Magpie. She'd been prickled, pinched, bumped, bashed and slooshed until her feathers were scraggly.

"I've never felt so miserable in all my life!" she said. "I never knew that a life of crime could lead to this. I'm going to give back all the things I've taken, and I promise never to steal again."

Surprisingly, Magpie managed to keep her promise. From that day on, every time she saw something shiny, it reminded her of the gummy gloop and made her shudder.

So, peace came to Boggart Hollow. The beasts lived together contentedly, helping one another the way that good neighbours should.

And since I haven't heard otherwise, they must all be living happily together still.

# Afterword

Most of the stories in this book are based on folk tales from around the world.

*Rabbit and the Wind, Slow and Steady* and *The Monster in the Well* are stories from Africa. *Fox's Revenge* and *Diddy Goat, Middy Goat and Great Goat* come from Scandanavia. *The Boggart Hollow Tug-of-War* is an Indian story, *The Rat Wedding* is Chinese. *How the Beasts came to Boggart Hollow* was taken from the stories of the Brothers Grimm and *Fox, the Crow and the Witch* is a mixture of one of Aesop's fables and a fairy tale by Charles Perrault.

The other stories are my own.